ALIEN DECEPTION

ANDREW MARK JAMESON

authorHOUSE®

AuthorHouse™ UK
1663 Liberty Drive
Bloomington, IN 47403 USA
www.authorhouse.co.uk
Phone: 0800.197.4150

Published by AuthorHouse 10/25/2016

ISBN: 978-1-5246-6539-5 (sc)
ISBN: 978-1-5246-6538-8 (e)

Chapter 1

Andrew was asleep in bed. It was the first week in December. Suddenly, Andrew awoke to hear 'voices' in his ears. The voices were female. They were saying "Don't be afraid – we are here to help you!" Over and over again the voices were saying the same thing. The voices grew in intensity and Andrew became uncomfortable. He reached over to nudge his alarm clock to check the time. It was 1.30 am!

Andrew suddenly realized that it was Saturday morning. Although very early it was Saturday morning – shopping day. Andrew listened into the voices again and they were still saying "Don't be afraid we are here to help you?" The voices were also saying "This is synthetic telepathy – do you have any questions? Andrew tried to say "no" in his head but couldn't seem to get a dialogue. It felt weird trying to communicate with the voices by thinking out loud. Andrew blurted out the words "No, no, no – I don't have any questions."

Andrew rolled around in bed, tossing and turning. Andrew likes his sleep so found it difficult being disturbed like this. It was 4.00 am. The voices stayed at a regular volume and were still saying "We are here to help you – don't be afraid" The voices went on to mention Carrie-Anne, Alison, Tracey and Tahir.

All these people were workmates of Andrew. They were all in his team at Her Majesty's Revenue and Customs, or HMRC. There Andrew was a tax officer. He dealt with customers over the telephone using a headset and desktop computer.

It was now 6.00 am and Andrew was wide awake. He decided to make a cup of tea. There's no way he could sleep now especially with caffeine in his system. As soon as it reached 8.00 am Andrew switched on Radio 4. Ahhh – it was the news. Just the same old news about the world and its problems.

When it got to 10.00 am Andrew got washed and dressed and headed out to the local supermarket. Saturday was his grocery shopping day. Just before Andrew ventured out of the door, the voices, which were ever present lowered slightly then said "We are in your head. You may find it strange and a little different". Andrew did find it strange but marched to the supermarket with his shopping bags and bought his groceries. After shopping he headed back to his flat which was situated in Bradford, West Yorkshire, England. It was a nice and comfortable one-bedroom flat situated just outside the city centre.

After putting his shopping away Andrew decided to have breakfast consisting of two slices of toast and a strong cup of coffee. He stayed in all weekend after that just listening to the radio. Except he did venture out on Sunday for Evening Praise at Sunbridge Road Mission Church in Bradford. He enjoyed Evening Praise because Pastor Phillips was an effervescent preacher. After he got home Andrew made an evening meal consisting of chips, beans, tomatoes and egg, with a couple of slices of bread. He washed it down with a cool refreshing glass of orange juice. A couple of hours later Andrew was in bed listening to Radio 4, setting his alarm for 7.30 am ready for work.

Andrew tossed and turned that night wondering how he was going to deal with this synthetic telepathy and cope with work at the same time.

7.30 am! The alarm fired off ! Andrew got washed and changed and had toast and a cup of coffee for breakfast. Andrew could feel his anger building because the voices would just not go away. The voices were commenting upon work and the last couple of days. Andrew could do no more. He rang 999 and spoke to the operator : "Police, how can we help?"

Andrew: "Im – er – hearing voices and they wont leave me alone"

Operator: "What are the voices saying?"

Andrew: "Its synthetic telepathy. The voices are saying its synthetic telepathy"

Operator: "Go on"

Andrew: "That's all I know at the moment. They just wont go away. What can I do?"

Operator: "Ill send someone round. Whats your address?"

Andrew: "Flat 11, Little Horton Lane, Bradford, BD4"

Operator: "The officer will be a few minutes. I have your phone number. Thank you, goodbye"

Andrew stood outside his flat awaiting an officer. He saw a police car cruise by slowly as if the officer was looking for something, an address maybe. Andrew flagged it down. It was PC Mollinson who stepped outside of his police car.

"Did you call us?"

Andrew: "Yes"

PC Mollinson: "Whats the problem?"

Andrew: "Im hearing voices and they wont go away. Its been going on for two days now!"

PC Mollinson: "Have you been drinking or taking illicit drugs over the weekend?"

Andrew: "No!"

PC Mollinson placed Andrew in the back of his car and stated he was being detained. Andrew didn't have time to lock up his flat. He was taken to Bradford South Police Station and processed. Andrew lay on a soft mattress in his cell. There was a young female police officer at the door sitting on a chair with the cell door ajar. Andrew felt calm but slightly intimidated. Andrew had never been in trouble with the police before.

After three hours Andrew was taken to Lynnefield Mount mental hospital as a voluntary patient. The police informed his employer. The hospital stank like chlorine. The only place of solace was his bedroom. There were some rowdy patients in there. They were mainly Asian, but this was Bradford.

Andrew befriended Saleem, a muslim. They listened to music, watched tv and played pool. Andrew looked forward to his meal times. They had breakfast, lunch, tea and dinner. Thursdays was his favourite day because it was fish and chips followed by peaches and cream for lunch.

The staff wore personal attack alarms. The alarms seemed to go off all the time. Andrew decided to paint a mural with Saleem. It took four days. Tomorrow was review day where all the doctors and psychiatric nurses would discuss Andrews case in open forum.

In the meantime Catherine, an Ops Manager from work visited Andrew at the mental hospital. It was general chit chat to see how he was. He said he was fine.

The big day had arrived. There were six nurses altogether and two doctors. They all sat round in a semi-circle. They asked Andrew if he was still hearing voices so he said "No". He said the voices had gone away. He served five more days then he was discharged.

Andrew went back to his flat by taxi. He paid the £5 fare then crept upstairs. Andrew had a community psychiatric nurse seconded to his case who visited him at his flat every two weeks. His name was Adam. Adam asked the nature of the voices. Andrew said they mainly comment on everyday stuff like going to the shops, or having a wash etc. Adam was a pleasant bloke who took no nonsense. Adam told Andrew to keep taking his medication of which Olanzapine was prescribed in tablet form. The medication didn't help at all.The synthetic telepathy carried on!

Chapter 2

Andrew decided to go back to work in Bradford. He went back to his old team with Carrie-Ann, Alison, Tracey and Tahir.

It was now Summer. The voices were still present but became nore abrasive in nature even stating "commit suicide". They would say this then refute it.

One day at work the "voices" appeared above Andrew's head at work. The voices could be heard distinctly by Andrew's co-workers. On one afternoon the voices were saying over and over again: "Andrew applied to be an astronaut…Andrew applied to be an astronaut…" Andrew did apply to be an astronaut the previous year before the voices. However Andrew received an e-mail from the European Space Agency saying he had failed in his application. He later learned that Major Tim Peake had got the vacancy.

Andrew's co-workers didn't say anything about the loud voices above his head at work. The voices were satellite directed. Except one afternoon, a friend of Andrew's called Shafaq did something seemingly ridiculous. As he was going for a break he stood up, flexed his biceps and said "Im an astronaut". He then went on his break. Andrew couldn't believe it. The whole contact centre was keeping quiet about the loud noise above Andrew's head but Shafaq, a close friend, managed to do that! Andrew was an unassuming individual who kept himself to himself and didn't tell anyone about his interest in applying to be an astronaut. Not only was Andrew surprised about Shafaq but also perplexed at the same time.

A few weeks later at work Andrew heard above his head, over and over again, "Andrew has just seen a jellyfish….. Andrew has just seen a jellyfish". Andrew had indeed seen a jellyfish in a national newspaper. There was a 600 foot long crop circle of a jellyfish with a photograph and a caption. One of the biggest crop circles ever found and it was in a Wiltshire wheat field. "Andrew has just seen a jellyfish…Andrew has just seen a jellyfish" was played constantly above his head at work. No one said a thing. Except one afternoon in the training suite, where the team was training for the new HMRC database to be installed, a colleague, Kaly said "Ive just seen a jellyfish". The training suite was quiet and Kaly's words seemed to echo. Andrew was sitting next to Kaly. He was perplexed and surprised at the same time just like when Shafaq stood up and said "Im an astronaut".

Every two weeks Andrew would go back to Conisbrough, near Doncaster which was a lovely little village in the heart of South Yorkshire. He would stay the weekend at his parent's house after travelling on a Friday night straight after work. He would get the six o' clock train from Bradford railway station and arrive in Conisbrough after a short bus journey from

Doncaster. He would arrive in Conisbrough, where his parent's lived about nine o' clock.

One particular weekend in Summer, Andrew travelled to Conisbrough. It was a red hot day, about 30 degrees celcius and a Saturday afternoon. The local farmers were cutting a nearby field of wheat. The combine was a yellow colour and there were two trailers parked at the fieldside. Andrew pulled up a chair outside and grabbed flask of coffee and some sandwiches and sat and watched the farmers. The combine was noisy. It traversed up and down the wheat field. The sky was blue and at the horizon Andrew could see a shimmer as the heat intensified. The voices made Andrew angry by ridiculing him. Andrew came to Conisbrough to escape the big city. The voices spoilt his afternoon.

After staying outside a good few hours Andrew made a firm decision. He decided to make a deliberate cry for help. Andrew went to bed at 9pm. When nightfall came, about 11pm, Andrew crept downstairs with a sleeping bag, some chocolate bars and a couple of energy drinks. He then went to the woods which was a half a mile away. He stayed in those woods. By now it was pitch black and there was no artificial light. This was the countryside and there was little light pollution.

By now it was morning and Andrew knew he would be missed. He lit a campfire using firelighters taken from Mum and Dads, and a cigarette lighter. He gathered up more firewood from the wood ready for putting on the fire. He ate another chocolate bar.

By now it was day four in the woods. He knew he'd be missed by his parents and colleagues at work. Andrew thought he heard a couple of men and a dog last night. Also the noisy clatter of South Yorkshire police's helicopter came overhead last night as though it was searching for something. Andrew's last night in the woods was calm. He could hear a couple of owls "twit-twoo… twit-twoo". He fell asleep. Andrew was down to his last chocolate bar and energy drink.

The next morning Andrew made another campfire. The weather was overcast. As he was sitting by the campfire an Alsation came crashing through the undergrowth and at Andrew, followed by a police officer. As his police issue radio crackled into life he said "Ah- Ive found you. Im going to radio into base. We've been looking for you for three whole days". At that point the police officer was joined by three other colleagues. One of them said "We were going to police the London G20 Summit but we got called out to you". They took my sleeping bag and rubbish from the woods and escorted me to an awaiting police van which was parked half a mile away. There were about twelve police officers near the van, and two patrol cars. The acting sergeant said "we are going to detain you", and took me in the van to St Catherines Hospital, Balby near Doncaster.

At the hospital Andrew looked in a mirror and saw four days of beard growth. He sighed, "Must get that beard shaved". Andrew was assessed by a panel of four psychiatric nurses and two doctors. Andrew told them he went to the woods as a cry for help. The voices would just not go away and they were present 24/7.

The hospital was a similar set up as to that one in Bradford. There was a set routine for meals. Andrew enjoyed his meal times. He noticed that this time the hospital had mainly white patients instead of Asian. There were various activities too including a walking group, a cookery group, a photography group, a gym and a learning suite. Andrew enjoyed the walking group. They walked around the spacious grounds of the hospital with its trees and plants and hedgeways. They took the same route for the photography group. The gym was held every morning and Andrew opted for the rowing machine and the treadmill. Andrew occasionally played pool and board games with the other patients.

During his stay, Andrew changed medication from Olanzapine to Quetiapine tablets. The Olanzapine was not working and was an anti-psychotic to help with paranoid schizophrenia, which Andrew was classed has suffering from.

Andrew began to research his condition whilst in St. Catherine's Hospital. He found a support network on Facebook and Twitter. He became friends with Tammy, Linda, Bedanta, Leila and a host of other victims of synthetic telepathy. On the social sites synthetic telepathy was also known as voice-to-skull technology (V2k), remote neural monitoring (rnm) and also Gangstalking. Basically satellites were putting voices into the heads of people across Europe and especially in America. Sleep deprivation was a part of this phenomenon. The "voices" would be put at high volume and 'buzzing' placed in the ears of the victims to prevent them going to sleep. Also part of this phenomenon included electronic dreams wherby a dream sequence would be placed at the target, or targeted individual. When Googling this phenomenon it was best to look under the heading ELECTRONIC HARASSMENT WEAPON EFFECTS.

There is a mini diagram of a woman with arrows pointing to various parts of her body labelled tinnitus, forced waking dreams, microwave hearing etc.

It was in St. Catherines hospital that Andrew was placed with the Early Interventions In Psychosis Service (EIT). This was lead by James who was introduced to Andrew in St. Catherines.

After three months Andrew was released from his 'section'. He went back out into the community. James of EIT visited Andrew every two weeks at his mother and father's house.

Weeks turned to months and eventually Andrew resigned from his position at HMRC in Bradford. This pained him somewhat since he really liked his job.

After two and a half years Andrew was passed to the Assertive Outreach Service (AOS) in the NHS. Jane was his mental health worker. His medication was changed from Quetiapine to Respiridone tablets. These were qiucklets which dissolved on the tongue instantly.

Another two years passed by and Andrew was placed on a depot injection called Clopixol. He was readmitted to hospital for a two month stay to assess 13

Clozapine. Jane thought this would be the magic bullet to put a stop to the voices. Unfortunately Andrew was allergic to Clozapine since it reacted with his red blood cells.

During this time AOS and Andrew devised an activity schedule. This comprised of a daily log of events to achieve. It started with 'activities for daily living' or ADLs. This was washing, getting a shave and changing in a morning. Then incorporated into the activity schedule were tasks eg lunch, daily workout, library, running, shopping, swimming, church, reading time, tea, tv and relaxation. This put Andrews life into perspective and gave him goals to achieve.

Andrew decided to research on the internet who could be behind the synthetic telepathy. He came across a variety of agencies but the one that caught his eye was DARPA. DARPA means Defence Advanced Research Projects Agency. It is an agency of the United States Department of Defense, responsible for the development of new technology for use by the military. It has an annual budget of millions of US dollars.

Chapter 3

Andrew spent his days following his activity schedule. Then – Eureka! Andrew came up with an amazing theory. Since Andrew believed in the existence of aliens he thought, why not. If humans could master synthetic telepathy then aliens could do it also.

The Quran contains scientific data which was only revealed to man in the latter century. The Quran is nearly 600 years old. It contains up-to-date scientific knowledge. When the prophet Muhammed revealed his wisdom through Divine Revelation was he talking to spirits in that cave he went to? No – he was being telepathized by a higher intelligence. That intelligence passed on the top scientific information as revealed in the Quaran. That intelligence must have been aliens.

Andrew's new theory was the following:

ARTIFICIAL + ENCYCLOPAEDIC = HIGHER

TELEPATHY KNOWLEDGE INTELLIGENCE

If humans could perform telepathy then aliens have definitely managed it. Andrew believes that aliens have visited our solar system for millennia based on the books he has read. They would have no doubt have visited Earth. It sound like something out of the X-Files but Andrew swears by it. UFOs have been sighted on Earth for thousands of years according to historical artefacts like the hieroglyphs inn ancient Egypt. UFOs have been captured on film and photography in the modern age. Andrew recently read a national newspapers report about photographs NASA has hidden for the past 30 years. The report said some respected professors and astronauts believe that there has been a cover-up by NASA. The report even claimed that when Apollo 11 landed on the moon it was being watched by aliens. A growing number of top scientists believe that Area 51 holds crashed UFOs. So aliens can telepathise human beings – contact has already been established.

Andrew believed humanity could be oblivious to the messages from extra-terrestrials because we have a limited view of the universe. Leading the hunt for alien life at the SETI institute in California, Dr Nathalie Cabrol has stated ET could be using technology unlike that being used on Earth. She stated "We have to use our imagination right now as to figure out what ET is doing?"

Contact has been established through alien technology.

Chapter 4

An artificial planet was orbiting a solar system 4.2 million light years away near Alpha Centauri. It was called Star 003 by the aliens. It was built over a period of 20 Earth years. It housed one billion aliens plus their craft. They lived a life of peace and prosperity. They even grew their own food on the artificial planet.

Meshat (pronounced Me-shay) was a district commander on the death star like planet. He oversaw all its functions including its telepathy hive, which telepathized all people on planet Earth. It was a major spy network. "Voices" weren't placed in the heads of the people on planet Earth but they were being watched! Only a select few people were chosen to receive "voices". These were known on Earth as clairvoyants. The clairvoyant's spirit guides were in fact aliens from Star 003. The aliens kept track of its clairvoyants 24/7.

Andrew decided one day to go to an evening of clairvoyance with medium, Stephen, at Doncaster. He called a taxi that brought him to the front door. It was £18 to get in on the door. The show was due to start at 7.30pm.

Andrew sat in the audience nervously tapping his feet. The room was full. Andrew sat next to the back row.

Stephen came on stage to the sound of music, and a round of applause. He was dressed in a tuxedo. He had blonde hair and was about 5' 9" tall. He had shiny black shoes.

"Good evening" said Stephen. "I hope you have an emotional, compelling and moving night. He shuffled to the front of the stage. "Lets see, do we have a Maria in the audience?" Someone put up her hand. She had sunglasses propped on her head and wore a light blue top. "Your cat has recently passed away hasn't he?"

"Yes, that's right" exclaimed Maria

"Its safe to say your cat has gone to cat heaven"

The audience gasped.

"Do we have a Freda in the audience tonight?" said Stephen clasping his handsFreda put up her hand. "Bert is looking down on you from heaven tonight, Freda. Hes really happy up there." The audience gasped. Freda pulled out her handkerchief and sniffled.

And so it went on.

On Star 003 Meshat was in charge of proceedings. He commissioned Stephen to be a clairvoyant when Stephen was in his teens.

Andrew sat patiently in the audience.

"And do we have an Andrew in the audience tonight?", said Stephen. Andrew put up his hand.

"Something magical and really special is going to happen in your life. I cant say when but it could be really soon." Andrew stated "Oh, thanks".The show went on for a good one and a half hours. Andrew sat there wondering what was going to happen. Andrew heard a programme on Radio 4 about clairvoyancy and two things struck him from the programme. One was that auntie Bessie from down the road always ends up on the same plane as Hitler and other evil characters. And the other was that the clairvoyant always talks about the mundane in life eg uncle Peter favourite soup is tomato soup. This programme mentioned that everyone ends up in Heaven. Andrew summised that there was no place in "Heaven" but that it was alien telepathy placing everyone on the same plane to the clairvoyants. Andrew also knew that aliens were secretly observing everyone from their base, including everyone in the audience tonight. They were telepathizing people and "hacking" their brains for information and through the use of supercomputers they were relaying this information back to Stephen, who was at work on the ground. Stephen just thought he was special having a spirit guide, and he earned a lot of money touring the country with his show. So tonight, without them knowing, Maria and Freda have been telepathized by the aliens and their memories mined for information. All the clairvoyants information was in the memories of the so called participants.

Andrew was a churchgoer. He goes to church every Sunday for Evening Praise at St. Peter's in Conisbrough.

Andrew worked out that there was no afterlife. The aliens were working some form of deception. Going to a clairvoyant gives us humans some form of belief in an afterlife. But Andrew had worked it out. Most religions call us to believe in some form of afterlife. This is central to Church of England philosophy, of which Andrew was a follower. Andrew thought howcouldthere be an afterlife since the aliens were using telepathy to trick people into thinking there was an afterlife.

Stephen shook hands with each and every member of the audience as they left the venue. Andrew muttered "Thank" to Stephen as he passed out of the doorway and into an awaiting taxi home.

Chapter 5

A few weeks had passed since Andrew went to see that clairvoyant. He was still waiting for something "wonderful" and "magical" to happen.

Andrew got up out of bed one morning and did his ADLs. Andrew switched on the radio. It was a programme about a police medium that helped find a body and lead to the arrest of the suspected murderer. Andrew knew instantly that that had been done using alien technology. The aliens, without consent, must be observing Earth from their platform. That's how the police medium could locate the body. The aliens had probably seen the murder and relayed information back to the police medium through his or her spirit guide.

Andrew suffered over the last two nights – sleep deprivation due to an infernal buzzing noise the synthetic telepathy perpetrators had directed at him.

Andrew researched Faraday bed canopies and Faraday cages on you-tube. The cage building was all about blocking the satellite signals using tin foil or another repellent. It meant using wooden supports and then placing the foil around the supports which could fit around a standard sized bed. On one you-tube clip it showed a constructed Faraday cage. The owner placed a standard radio in the cage with it being tuned to a station playing music. They closed the door on the cage and the radio went to static. They opened the door and the radio played music. They closed the door again and the radio went to static. They opened the door again and the music came back on. This controlled test showed that the Faraday cage could block radio signals. The controlled test was also done with a mobile phone. When the cage was closed the signal bars went from 5 bars to nil bars. When the cage was opened the bars went back to full strength. Andrew decided against building a cage but opted instead to buying a Faraday bed canopy from Amazon for £900.

Andrew eagerly awaited his purchase. It arrived within 5 days. He opened his Faraday bed canopy and suspended it, a mosquito-type net, above his bed. He used a drill to drill four holes for the ceiling hooks, then attached the mosquito-type net to the ceiling. He placed a radio in the canopy. It still played music therefore it didn't stop radio signals. Using a test with a mobile phone the number of bars went from five to one. The signal wasn't being fully blocked. Andrew sat under the canopy for half an hour. It didn't block the synthetic telepathy, the main reason for purchasing the canopy.

Andrew dismantled the canopy after 2 weeks since it was cumbersome to manage climbing in and out of bed.

Chapter 6

Helen was only 16 years old. She was a pretty girl with shoulder length black curly hair. She was of slim build. Her stable was only a 10 minute walk away. As she opened the gate to her paddock, Milly, her horse, whinneyed. Helen strapped on the saddle and riding tac. Helen was in her jodhpurs and a light blue sweater. It was a warm Autumn day and her ride was going to be pleasant. As she mounted Milly, she gently patted her on the back "Good girl, Milly. Go on girl". Helen tapped the horse with her legs and held the reigns tight. Off she moved.

Over dale, stream, mud and bracken Helen saw the world go by.

After Helen finished her ride she took off the horses tac and then cleaned out the stable. The stable ponged a bit due to the manure. She fed Milly then walked the ten minute journey home.

"Just in time for tea!" Helen's mum said as she dished out peas, pie and chips. This was Helen's favourite meal. After the meal Helen went to her bedroom and changed into her onesie. The one she normally sleeps in. She came running downstairs and ate her meal with her mother, Ann and father, John. Ann and John had been married twenty years and Heleln was her only daughter. Helen was a loner and had one close friend called Sarah.

"Mum, Im going to my room" said Helen

"Okay" said Ann

Helen turned on her tv in her bedroom. There was a game show on and she watched it. After the game show she read a book. The time was 9.30pm and so Helen decided it was time for bed. She brushed her teeth then combed her hair then went to bed in her onesie. The bedroom window was open and she could hear the gentle breeze outside. Helen soon became sleepy and started to doze off.

A gust of wind blew outside. Helen was woozy when she heard it. Voices in her ears: "We care about you and we love you". Helen was perplexed. She lay in bed transfixed at the ceiling. "Helen, my name is Morgan. Im going to be your spirit guide from now on. I will guide you and help you. When you get up tomorrow morning I want you to tell your mother she is going to have a significant win on the lottery next week. Will you do that for me" said Morgan the spirit guide. After all Helen was now fully awake and became quite excited "What do you look like?" said Helen. Morgan said "I'm a thirty year old male with crystal blue eyes and shoulder length blonde hair. Ill send you an image. Just close your eyes for a moment". Helen closed her eyes and saw the image of Morgan. "You look like a hunk to me" said Helen. "Anyway I'll tell my mum tomorrow about the lottery win". Morgan said "I'm going now I'll speak to you at the same time tomorrow night. Bye"

"Bye" said Helen "Bye"

Helen went to sleep.

Meanwhile on Star 003 Meshat had commissioned Helen to receive a spirit guide. She had been observed since the age of fourteen years old. She is deemed suitable to have a spirit guide.

Andrew knew that aliens were telepathizing humans and they could pick out whoever they wanted to be a clairvoyant. The aliens had vast supercomputers that could even predict future events. These events were sometimes relayed to their 'victim' from their spirit guide.

Helen got up and felt refreshed after a good nights sleep. She got washed and changed ready for school. It was her first year at doing A-levels. She chose history, English, biology and general studies. She was doing really well at biology.

"Mum" she said "I've got a spirit guide called Morgan"

"Don't be silly" said Ann

"And you are going to win on the lottery this coming week" said Helen

"Really" said Ann

"I saw a picture of him in my head… of Morgan. He has blonde hair and blue eyes…he's good looking" said Helen

"Really. Now eat your breakfast and I'll run you to school" said Ann.

Helen fastidiously ate her breakfast. She then brushed her teeth then went to school in her mum's car.

On arriving at school Helen didn't mention the spirit guide to a soul. She couldn't wait for bedtime to see if he would come back.

Helen arrived back home from school and got changed into her riding gear. She went for a brisk ride on Milly. The weather was fine. She didn't have to clean out the stables since she only did it once a week.

Helen went to bed at 10 pm. Morgan, her spirit guide spoke to her as promised. Morgan was really an alien telepathizing Helen but Helen didn't know this. Morgan did in fact have blue eyes and blonde hair and was humanoid. He spoke perfect English. He spoke to Helen about her day and her teachers at sixth form.

It was Friday and Ann was excited. She had just won £5,000 on a lottery scratchcard. Helen's message came to mind.

At tea time Ann mentioned her win in front of Helen, and John her father. Helen couldn't believe it! Ann couldn't believe it!

"Dad" said Helen with a sad expression on her face "You're not going to believe it but don't go to golf this week because there is going to be an accident".

John said "Don't talk rubbish, Im going".

The hospital rang on Thursday afternoon. Helens dad had suffered serious whiplash injuries from a minor car crash after travelling to golf.

Chapter 7

Andrew received a reply to his e-mail to the Home Office. His original e-mail mentioned the abuse he keeps receiving from the synthetic telepathy, and the sleep deprivation techniques applied to him. A civil servant suggested writing to the Investigatory Powers Tribunal Service. They look into claims of human rights abuses involving modern technology. It is usually associated with GCHQ, MI5 or MI6 eavesdropping on electronic communications and then prosecuting if there are any terrorist links. Andrew thought it might be worth a try to see who could be behind the synthetic telepathy; who the perpetrators are. Andrew eagerly awaited his post.

Meanwhile on Star 003 the aliens kept good track of Helen, and Stephen the clairvoyant, and virtually everybody else on Earth.

Andrew went on the internet. There was a post on Facebook from Tammy: "Over 1.1k comments and 4.6k shares. Yeah, I think we have a problem with Electromagnetic Weapons illegally torturing countless Americans and countless people around the world". The post was attached to the following: "Electromagnetic weapons (synthetic telepathy) are being used to illegally torture and enslave countless Americans. This is truly the greatest threat to the survival of the USA since the Civil War, because the stealth weapons are capable of subverting the rule of law. The criminals behind it..."

Andrew sighed. Yet another negative post.

Andrew picked up his local paper. In it was a piece about the Chinese designing and using a 1640 foot dish sweeping the skies for signals from alien galaxies. It's the worlds largest radio telescope!Andrew met his mental health nurse and had his depot injection of Clopixol (400 mg) in his buttocks. The mental health team now stated it was treatment resistant schizophrenia. Obviously Andrew knew different that it was satellite directed synthetic telepathy or electronic harassment. He also went on Facebook and saw a piece from one of the main proponents of synthetic telepathy. This guy had helped develop synthetic telepathy. He said in his post that the US Government was doing this to worldwide citizens and that the weapons were deemed "voice of God" weapons. He said that certain citizens were being tortured by these "voice of God" weapons. The people that do this are hard to find and they hide in the most darkest of crevices. Synthetic telepathy is sometimes called 'remote neural monitoring'.

Andrew dedided to go on the internet. He grabbed a bakewell tart and a cup of coffee and opened up files about "UFOs and aliens". He sipped his coffee. Andrew saw that as long ago as ancient Egypt in 1480 BC there were sightings of UFOs. Hieroglyphs, or picture writing, from this period describe foul smelling fiery circles hovering over the court of Egyptian king Pharoah Thutmos III. Egyptian paintings also show weird creatures with huge eyes that some people think are drawings of aliens from other worlds. Andrew immediately thought of the so called "greys" which had huge hairless heads and big black almond –shaped eyes. Andrew read on: In Australia, 5000 year old Aboriginal cave paintings depict spooky giant eyed beings. Paintings from 15th -century Europe shoe weird globes lighting up the sky. Andrew thought aliens may have landed on Earth. Perhaps the human race is descended from aliens. Andrew thought that the "missing link" in our anthropological make-up could be due to the fact that aliens genetically engineered our predecessors. We all could have alien blood.

During World War II aircraft pilots in Europe and the Far East saw mysterious coloured lights in the skies during their missions. They were named "foo fighters". These balls of light were capable of impressive aerial manoeuvres. Andrew knew they were aliens and not ball lightning or hallucinations by fearful pilots.

The modern UFO era began in 1947. American airline pilot Kenneth Arnold tracked nine objects moving at high speed over the Cascade Mountains, Washington, USA. He said they moved like a "saucer would if you skipped it across the water". Soon afterwards newspapers were calling them "flying saucers". Within weeks hundreds of similar objects were being reported.

Andrew read on: In the 1960s tv became popular with alien characters like the Klingons in Star Trek and the daleks in Dr Who. In the late 1970s the Star Wars movies took off. Other popular movies included "Close Encounters of the Third Kind (1977) and ET: The Extraterrstrial (1982).

There are modern day UFO sightings like the one made by Jack, aged 11, over Loughton in Essex. He used his family camers to take a crisp photo of an oval-shaped UFO in the Summer sunshine. Up to 70,000 UFO sightings are reported worldwide each year. It is thought that nearly half of Americans believe in UFOs.

Andrew made himself another cup of coffee and ate a packet of crisps. Andrew was really enthralled with all the alien stuff on the internet. He came upon a UFO sighting dating back to 1996 where a huge mothership, the size of a football stadium was spotted by 22 people along the Klondike Highway in Canada's Yukon Territory. Sightings of motherships are rare. More commonly, people report smaller discs, crescents and triangles in the sky. Many UFO reports are of fast moving objects that can change direction in an instant. No human craft could do this since it would require technology beyond our understanding.

The mothership reminded Andrew of the film Independence Day and also the 2016 film Independence Day : Resurgence where motherships came to attack Earth.

Chapter 8

Andrew moved on from researching UFO sightings to "little green men". Aliens may come in all sorts of forms. In eyewitness reports, common features appear again and again. Greys are described as short, hairless beings with pear-shaped heads and large, dark almond-shaped eyes. They are usually shorter than humans and have no visible ears. They usually communicate via telepathy.

Reptilian aliens are thought to be cold blooded. They might have webbed fingers and toes and scaly skin.

Then there are the ones which look like humans. They are about six foot in height and have hair and slender bodies.

Andrew researched aliens from film. The hairy Chewbacca is a co-pilot of the Millebnium Falcon spaceship in Star Wars. Jabba the Hutt is a sloth like alien in the Star Wars franchise. He controls his criminal empire from a palace on the desert world of Tattooine.

The Xenomorphs from the movie Alien (1979) and its sequels are predatory creatures. Then there are the mechanised daleks from the Dr Who tv series.

Finally The Hitchikers Guide to the Galaxy tv series had a grumpy race of the Vogans.

32

Andrew could see that there was a large scope of alien races and agendas. He switched off his internet and went to bed, thinking about the many alien beings.

Andrew got up Sunday morning, got dressed and went to church. It was churches together this Sunday with a bring and share Sunday lunch for Harvest Festival. After singing a few hymns and watching the church choir Andrew went across to the dining hall where four sets of tables were laid out with their cutlery. Enough for about 120 people. Andrew sat next to Johnny, a good friend, and ate his bring-and-share lunch. There was a table quiz and Andrew contributed to some of the answers. His team came runner-up with 15 out of a possible of 20 correct answers. After saying goodbye to Johnny, Andrew made his way home.

Andrew logged onto the internet and began more research into aliens and UFOs. His own synthetic telepathy was at low volume at the minute. He read: In Germany in 1561 in Nuremberg the local paper the gazette reported that the dawn sky was filled with huge cylinders, globes of various colours and blood-red crosses. All were constantly moving in what appeared to be a battle in the sky.

In a book by Erich von Daniken(1968) he claimed that aliens had long been visiting Earth. These aliens had bred with humans too. Andrew agreed with this snippet of information. He believed that Neanderthalls had been genetically developed to create the modern day homo-sapiens and that's why there was a gap in the anthropomorphological records. He believed in evolution but also in genetic manipulation.

Andrew read on : In 329 BC, the army of Alexander the Great was crossing a river when shiny silver shields swooped down towards the soldiers creating panic. Several years later whilst attacking the Phoenician city of Tyre, a glowing beam destroyed the city's walls.

In 1492, Christopher Columbus and a crew member aboard his ship, the Santa Maria, saw a flickering light that moved up and down in the sky. It reappeared several times during the night. It was spotted just before Columbus sighted land on his voyage of the Atlantic Ocean.

Andrew got another coffee and researched more. He came upon alien hunters who were there to contain any UFO activity before it spread panic. There were the Men in Black. These wore dark suits and visited witnesses to UFO sightings over the years. Some speculate these were Government agents trying to keep UFO reports undercover. In 1966, reporter John Murphy was to claim that he was visited at his radio station in Pennsylvania, USA by two Men in Black. They wanted to talk to him about photographs he had taken of a glowing object that crashed in the woods. It could have been a UFO.

Andrew dedided to go for a run. He quickly changed into his tracksuit bottoms and ahirt and trainers. He also attached his Walkman to a utility belt then set off. He ran through open countryside and woodland. The temperature was 15 degrees which was normal for early Autumn.

When he got back from his 45 minute run he took a shower then changed back into his normal clothes; jeans and a jumper. He made himself another cup of coffee then logged onto the internet. He decided to research alien abductions:

- Encounter of the first kind : person comes within 150m of a UFO

- Encounter of the second kind : person sees close up evidence of a UFO

- Encounter of the third kind : person witnesses aliens as well as a UFO

- Encounter of the fourth kind : person taken on board a UFO

- Encounter of the fifth king : face-to-face communication with aliens

Perhaps the most well known UFO abduction case was that of Betty and Barney Hill on September 19th 1961. On that evening the couple were driving along a deserted mountain road in New Hampshire, USA when suddenly a bright object dropped down towards them. They didn't remember much of that incident immediately but drove home as fast as they could.

Betty's memories came flooding back over a period of a few nights. Short, hairless beings with large heads had taken the Hills into their spacecraft and subjected them to a medical examination.

Andrew came across a bewilderingly high number of UFO incidents:

- The Day Family

    35

    October 27, 1974

    Aveley, Essex

- Garry Wood and Colin Wright

    17 August 1992

    A70 near Harpering Reservoir

    Lothian District, Scotland

- Philip Spencer

    December 1, 1987

    Ilkley Moor

    West Yorkshire

- George and Amanda Philips

    August 30, 1982

    Cleveland

    Tyne and Wear

- Douglas Tams

    June 5, 1974

    Staffordshire

- James Millen

  September6, 1990

  Fleet, Dorset

Retired landscape gardener James Millen and his wife Pam were on a camping holiday at West Farm near Fleet in Dorset.

James was 54 at the time and he and Pam had driven down from their home in Putney, London to the campsite which overlooks Chesil Beach.

West Farm camp, site was less busy than usual. At night, James noticed a few golden, orange balls of light, rising and falling in the sky.

It transpired that James had lost a few hours of time that night. Also James' camera lens was covered in a strange lime/mortar mixture. Could James have been abducted?

Andrew got himself another cup of coffee and a sandwich and continued researching:

On December 26th, 1980, a UFO is spotted close to a military airbase near Rendlesham Forest. Staff Sargeant Jim Penniston was a member of the Rendlesham patrol who saw the UFO. Two nights later the deputy base commander Lieutenant Colonel Charles Halt took a second patrol out and spotted flashing red lights in the sky.

In the 1970s mysterious patterns of flattened vegetation appeared in farmers fields worldwide. They were given the name "crop circles" and they became more elaborateas time went on. Many people thought they were due to alien activity until mischievous humans admitted to doing them.

A top secret military airbase located in the Nevada desert, USA, is the source of many UFO rumours. The US Air Force runs Area 51. It specialises in developing new military aircraft. Shrouded in mystery, some people speculate that alien craft have been recovered to that site and reverse engineered. Also secret meetings with extraterrestrials have taken place there.

A famous story of a UFO crash that took place in Roswell, New Mexico in 1947. It began when a local farmer had found some unusual materials 70 miles from the Roswell Army Air Field. There was speculation that it was a crashed disc, but media outlets said it was a weather balloon. The story wouls not go away.

The "Goldilocks Zone" is the name given to places in space where the conditions are just right for life as we know it like that on Earth. It comes from the tale "Goldilocks and the Three Bears" where Goldilocks, a little girl tries porridge from the bears. One is too hot, the other too cold and the third is just right. Andrew read : the following are some places outside our solar system with planets and moons within the Goldilocks Zone:

- Gliese 581: two planets that are orbiting this star are "super-earths". Could life exist there?
- 55 Cancri : there are 5 planets around this star. The fifth planet is within the Goldilocks Zone. It is largely composed of gas but might have moons orbiting it that are large enough to support life.

Some scientists still think that life could exist on Mars. Satellite images show that Mars probably had water running on the planet. Andrew quickly went to his drawer and found an newspaper cutting showing an anomaly on Mars. It showed a picture of a huge cross and the ruins of a temple. Alien hunters have called it "a significant religious discovery". The images, beamed from NASAs Curiosity Rover show also seemingly carved stones. Paranormal investigator Scott C Waring said: "This is a very unusual find and probably a significant discovery for those who are religious. I would bet big money that this is a full-size cross. Near the cross there are the ledges of a beautifully carved roof that has since caved in."

In February 2016 Curiosity sent pictures of a face that enthusiasts claim is an ancient Martian sculpture, not dissimilar to the Mars "face" that is well recognised within the UFO community.

Andrew went back to the internet. He supped his coffee which was going cold. Under the search bar : "Searching for Extraterrestrials" an international project that involves scanning space with giant radio telescopes is being carried out by SETI; the "Search for Extraterrestrial Intelligence". This is because radio waveare easier to detect than light.

In 1972 and 1973 scientists launched the Pioneer 10 and 11 space probes to explore the solar system. These unmanned craft carried golden plaques showing human figures and a diagram of the Earth's place within our solar system. This is in case aliens found the information and were interested in our planet.

Andrew read on. We haven't discovered any alien signals so far. Truly advanced races might be using energy sources we can't presently detect.

Andrew thought of synthetic telepathy. On Earth DARPA or such like are using satellite directed microwave radiation for their "effects" on targeted individuals. Aliens may be using a more sophisticated energy source that may transmit "voices" and "images" into human subjects. Clairvoyants could be at the leading edge in cutting-edge alien technology. Scientists on Earth can control satellites up to 450 million miles away from Earth. God knows how far alien technology can reach.

Chapter 9

Helen turned 18 years old. She got a riding hat and a pair of riding gloves for her birthday. She also received a few cards and well wishes on Facebook. She won a place at Southampton University to study psychology. But Helen decided to take a gap year in her studies before embarking on her course.

Helen had visited a couple of clairvoyant sessions of Stephen's. She struck up a working relationship with Stephen.

Andrew was walking down the street when he saw an A4-sized poster advertising £15 for entry into a clairvoyant show at the local pub. It was hosted by Helen and Stephen together. Andrew pulled out a pen and wrote down the time and date for the show with the intention of going. Andrew, on the same journey, came across Islamic Vision giving out leaflets named "Life After Death". He took one home.

Andrew took out that yellow pamphlet. He had a sip of his tea. "Life After Death: the question whether there is life after death does not fall under the jurisdiction of science as science is only concerned with the classification and analysis of sense data..." Andrew disagreed already since his belief was that "spirits" are the result of aliens telepathizing humans and making them believe in the "spirit" world. The afterlife is purely scientific. Whatever alien technology is it is definitely performing in the scientific field if it could be measured. Electronic harassment, or synthetic telepathy is within the scientific field since it is controlled by satellite directed microwave radiation to the targeted individual.

The pamphlet carried on… "All the prophets of God called their people to worship God and to believe in life after death. They laid so much emphasis of the belief in life after death that even a slight doubt in it meant denying God and made all other beliefs meaningless. We also know that these prophets of God were greatly opposed by their people, mainly on the issue of life after death as their people thought it impossible". Andrew knew it was impossible even though he was a Christian follower. That Sunday the vicar proclaimed "We all as Christians are going to Heaven where we will praise God at all times!" Andrew knew this couldn't be true but he kept his mouth shut. The yellow pamphlet went on : "But in spite of opposition the prophets won so many sincere followers. The question arises what made those followers forsake the established belief of their forefathers. They could be at risk of alienation in their own communities. They used their faculties of heart and mind and realised the truth. God has given man consciousness. It is this consciousness that guides man regarding realities that cannot be verified through sensory data. Andrew took another sip of his tea. Andrew knew Jehovah's Witnesses didn't believe in life after death. Andrew spoke to Ian regularly, in passing, about religion on Thursdays.

Ian was an ambassador for the Jehovah's Witness movement. Andrew had thought about becoming a Jehovah's Witness but it meant throwing away all that he had become familiar with. The yellow pamphlet went on: "The explanation that the Quaran (and the Bible) gives about the necessity of life after death is what moral consciousness of man demands. Actually, if there is no life after death, the very belief in God becomes irrelevant or even if one believes in God, that would be an unjust and indifferent God, having once created man and not concerned with his fate. Surely, God is just". Andrew immediately thought of Jehovah's Witnesses who don't believe in life after death. They have a good following and their people are okay.

The pamphlet went on: "The belief in life after death not only guarantees success in the hereafter but also makes this world full of peace and happiness by making individuals most responsible and dutiful in their activities.

Think of the people of Arabia. Gambling, wine, tribal feuds, plundering and murdering were there main traits when they had no belief in life after death. But as soon as they accepted the belief in one God and life after death they became the most disciplined nation of the world. They gave up their vices, helped eachother in times of need, and settled all their disputes on the basis of justice and equality.

Thus there are some very convincing reasons to believe in life after death:

Firstly: all the prophets of God have called their people to believe in it

Secondly: whenever a human society is built on the basis of this belief, it has been the most ideal and peaceful society, free of social and moral evils

Thirdly: history bears witness that whenever this belief is rejected collectively by a group of people in spite of repeated warning of the prophet, the group has been punished by God even in this world

Fourthly: moral, aesthetic and rational faculties of man endorse the possibility of life after death

Fifthy: God's attributes of Justice and Mercy have no meaning if there is no life after death.

Andrew put the whole pamphlet into perspective. He knew aliens were allowing humans to believe in life after death through their clairvoyants. And he also knew that Jehovah's Witnesses lead a saintly life even though they don't believe in life after death.

Andrew went to another church event. It was held fro men. It was an evening of playing football, badminton, table tennis and table football with a quiz and food thrown in. Andrew really enjoyed it. It started at 7.30 pm and didn't finish until 11.00 pm.

Another Christmas came and went. It snowed heavily. Andrew spent it with his family. Andrew had three sisters and one brother. They had a buffet at his brothers house in Doncaster.

One day Andrew went to the Christmas choir service at St Peters Church, and the Christmas carol service. He remembers the overhead projector showing the words to sing and also some brightly coloured pictures. The church was packed. When "O Little Town of Bethlehem" came up there was a picture of the manger and Mary and Joseph. There was also a brilliant white star above the manger. Andrew immediately thought of a book he had read stating that the star could have been a UFO, and that the virgin birth of Jesus could have been alien technology which fertilized Mary.

Andrew was still waiting for his "majical and fantastical" event to happen. It had been promised by Helen and Stephen the clairvoyants a handful of times now.

Andrew hadn't long to wait.

Chapter 10

Meanwhile on Star 003, Meshat had authorised the abduction of Andrew. It was going to be tonight.

Andrew was asleep in bed. His voices were on low. Suddenly he awoke to a strange low humming noise coming from above the roof of the house. It was pitch black and the time was 2 am. Suddenly a white traction beam lit up Andrew's bedroom. Andrew was fully awake. The beam elevated Andrew through the rooftop and into a flying saucer. The saucer was about 50 metres in diameter.

Once inside Andrew found himself on a soft bed surrounded by three 'normal' looking aliens and about six greys. The normal looking aliens wore skin- tight military style uniforms.

"Hello, Im Zena" said the female alien. "We are taking you to our death star outside Alpha Centauri. Have a look round our craft. We have been observing you for a long time, and we know you have a good insight into our lives from the books and videos you have seen". Andrew smiled. Zena said "Come have a look. This is our hyperdrive. We can move from cruising speed to faster than light travel. We can travel instantly. See this is our joystick. It is floating and can be altered a full 360 degrees to change the saucers path in microseconds.This is the saucers computer. All command are carried out instantly as if the alien pilots and the craft are one being. Zena said pointing" This is the friction absorber which channels the heat caused by friction when the saucer travels through space. And finally this is the inertia damper. It protects the crew from g-forces when our pilots rapidly increase speed or change direction.

And while I have been showing you round the spacecraft we have been travelling faster than the speed of light. Can you see" sais Zena "That's our home!". It was a huge sphere, the size of Earth, with lights, archways and flying saucers coming and going. Andrew was awestruck. Amazed! Zena said, "Alpha Centauri is our solar system. Its similar to Earth's solar system.

After cruising around the sphere the flying saucer headed back to England, and South Yorkshire. A traction beam placed Andrew back into bed. "Goodbye said Zena, goodbye". Andrew waved from his bed.

Andrew sat up in bed having had the most "majical" experience. Also he noticed that the synthetic telepathy had been switched off. It must have been because Andrew came out of range of Earths satellites.

Andrew got up the next day. He celebrated by having a meal with his mum and dad. After all, Helen and Stephen were right in their prediction.

Printed in the United States
By Bookmasters